Ririwha: Guardian of the Northern Harbour

A Modern Pūrākau - A Story Inspired by Aotearoa's Landscape

Author's Note

This is a work of fiction inspired by the landscape and storytelling traditions of Te Tai Tokerau (Northland), Aotearoa New Zealand. While it draws on the style of traditional pūrākau (Māori legends), all characters, events, and specific cultural details are fictional creations. The place names have been modified to honor the real locations without claiming to represent their actual histories or legends.

Readers interested in the true histories and pūrākau of Northland are encouraged to connect with local iwi, visit regional museums, and learn from those who hold mana whenua (territorial rights) over these lands.

This story explores themes of kaitiakitanga (guardianship), balance with nature, and the consequences of greed. Universal themes that speak to our current environmental challenges.

A Glossary of Te Reo Māori Terms can be found near the end of this book.

Aotearoa Giants

Table of Contents

Part One: Te Ao Mārama - The World of Light

In a time before time was counted, when mountains walked and stars spoke, there stood a guardian so ancient that even the wind had forgotten her first name. The people called her **Ririwha** and she was magnificent.

From her place in the ocean, Ririwha watched over everything. Her eyes swept across the sparkling waters of the northern bays, across the golden sands where the sea met the land, all the way to the scattered jewels of the eastern islands. She stood 2,930 metres tall, her shoulders draped in clouds, her feet planted firmly on the ocean floor. When the sun rose, it painted her western face gold. When storms came, she turned her back to shield the bays from the worst of the wind.

She had stood there for more than a millennium. Long enough to watch forests grow, die, and grow again. Long enough to see the first waka arrive on these shores. Long enough to know that guardianship was not about power, but about patience.

Beyond Ririwha's ancient boundaries lay a vast freshwater lake, pristine and deep. The people called it **Whai-roa-moana**, the long-pursued waters. Its surface was so clear you could see the silver flash of tuna (eels) twenty feet down. So calm that the moon's reflection lay upon it like a pearl on dark cloth. This was home.

On the shores of Whai-roa-moana lived Ririwha's children: her daughter **Kaimana** and her son **Tiaki-rangi**.Kaimana had inherited her mother's height and her father's fierce heart. She stood tall enough to pluck ripe berries from the tallest kahikatea trees, strong enough to carry a full-grown moa under each arm. Kaimana had a partner named **Tū-tara** or Standing-Spine. He was the chief of their village. His people loved him for his fair judgments and his thundering laugh. His back was broad enough to carry the troubles of his people, and his hands were gentle enough to weave flax into fishing nets that caught only what was needed.

Tū-tara had two wives, as was the way of great chiefs. Kaimana, fierce and loyal, who stood by his left side. And **Hāwera**, Echo-Sound. Who was small and quick and clever, who stood by his right.

But it was Tiaki-rangi whom the birds loved most.

Tiaki-rangi and the Sky Gardens

Tiaki-rangi had seen nine hundred and seventy-three winters. His hands were steady. His voice was soft. Every morning, before the sun cracked the horizon, he walked to the great **manu whare**, the bird sanctuaries.

These were not cages. No, they were something far older and stranger.

Imagine domes of stone and vine, each one half a kilometre wide, stretching up until their peaks disappeared into the low-hanging clouds. The frames were woven from **kareao** (supplejack), twisted so tight they'd lasted a thousand years.

The walls were living things. **Harakeke** (flax) growing so thick that not even the smallest rat could squeeze through, all draped in **tataramoa** (bush lawyer), whose thorns were as long as your finger.

Inside these vast sanctuaries lived the birds of old Aotearoa.

Hōkioi (Haast's eagles) with wingspans wider than a waka, whose shadows passed over the forest like clouds. **Kererū** (wood pigeons) so fat they could barely fly, their feathers shimmering blue-green in the filtered light. **Ruru-whekau** (laughing owls) whose calls echoed through the valleys like human laughter. And the **kiwi**. Oh, the kiwi!, thousands of them, rustling through the leaf litter, their calls filling the night air with music.

On the forest floor below the domes wandered the **moa**. These great birds, taller than Tiaki-rangi himself, moved like living shadows through the moss-covered rocks and fern groves. They fed on the berries that fell from above, on the shoots that grew in the clearings, on the leaves that drifted down like rain.

Tiaki-rangi did not farm them. That would be disrespectful. Instead, he protected them. He maintained the structures his tūpuna (ancestors) had built. He repaired the torn vines where curious hōkioi had tested their strength. He cleared the streams that trickled down from the mountains so the birds always had fresh water.

And in return, the birds gifted him their eggs.

Not all of them, of course. Just the extras. The ones laid in abundance during good seasons. Tiaki-rangi had taught the hōkioi a clever game: they would fetch eggs from the smaller birds' nests and place them in a large carved bowl at the centre of each dome. In return, Tiaki-rangi left them haunches of dried moa meat and fresh-caught ika (fish).

It was a partnership. A conversation between species that had lasted longer than any human could remember.

Each morning, Tiaki-rangi would collect what had been gifted. He'd crack six or seven of the enormous eggs into a heated stone bowl and scramble them with kawakawa leaves and a pinch of sea salt. The smell alone could wake the village.

"E Tiaki-rangi!" Tū-tara would boom across the village. "Are you feeding us or trying to make us jealous?"

"Both, perhaps," Tiaki-rangi would reply, his eyes crinkling with amusement. "Come, there's enough for everyone. There's always enough."

This was the way of things. This was balanced. This was **kaitiakitanga**.

But balance, like all precious things, is fragile.

The Gathering Storm

To the west, beyond the village, beyond the gardens and the bird sanctuaries, rose a range of mountains that scraped the belly of the sky. The people rarely spoke of those mountains, and when they did, they lowered their voices.

For in those mountains lived **Maunga-kēhua**, the Ghost Mountain.

He was old. Older than Ririwha. Older than memory. His body was so vast it formed seven separate peaks, each one a spike along his serpentine spine. His skin was thick as ancient stone, covered in scales that had calcified into armor plates over the millennia. Moss grew in the crevices. Trees sprouted from his back. Rivers ran through the channels of his body.

He slept. Mostly.

But lately, he has been having restless dreams.

Maunga-kēhua had children, hundreds of them. Smaller taniwha, each one still large enough to swallow a moa whole, with the same jewel-faceted eyes as their father. Eyes that saw in spectrums humans couldn't imagine. Eyes that could freeze prey with a glance under the right moon.

For generations, these taniwha had hunted carefully. They took only what they needed. They respected the **tapu** (sacred restrictions) that maintained the balance.

But as time passed, as decades blurred into centuries, the children forgot. They grew greedy. They hunted more than they needed. They taught their children to do the same. Soon, the forests nearest the western mountains grew quiet. The streams ran empty. The tapu was broken.

Now they were hungry. Truly, desperately hungry.

And hunger makes monsters of anyone.

The taniwha began raiding the bird sanctuaries at night. They would tear through the tataramoa walls, their thick hides impervious to thorns. They'd gorge themselves on eggs, on kiwi, on anything they could catch. Then they'd slither back to their caves, leaving destruction in their wake.

Tiaki-rangi would wake to find his careful repairs torn apart again. He'd find feathers scattered like snow. He'd hear the cries of frightened birds.

"We cannot keep living this way," Kaimana said one evening as she helped her brother repair a torn section of vine wall. "They're taking more than their share. They're breaking the covenant."

"I know," Tiaki-rangi replied quietly, his hands working the kareao with practiced ease. "But what can we do? We cannot fight an army of taniwha."

"Then we speak to their father," Tū-tara said, approaching with Hāwera beside him. "We remind Maunga-kēhua of the old agreements. Of respect. Of balance."

"And if he doesn't listen?" Hāwera asked. She was the smallest of them, barely ten feet tall, but her mind was the sharpest.

Tū-tara was quiet for a long moment. Then he placed one massive hand on his wife's shoulder, and one on Kaimana's. "Then we trust in Ririwha. She has watched over us for a thousand years. She will not abandon us now."

But Ririwha was far away, out in the deep ocean, her back to the land. And she did not yet know that danger was circling her family like sharks in dark water.

High above, the moon was waxing. Growing fuller. Growing red.

In seven days, it would be time.

Part Two: Te Pō - The Night of Shadows

The red moon rose like a wound in the sky.

Tiaki-rangi saw it first as he made his evening rounds. He stopped, his hand still on a half-tied knot of supplejack, and stared upward. The moon hung low and huge, swollen with strange light. It was the colour of old blood, of pōhutukawa flowers, of the warning sky before a storm.

A **maramataka** (lunar calendar) moon. A moon of power.

"Brother?" Kaimana's voice came from behind him. She'd felt it too, that electric tension in the air, like the moment before lightning strikes.

"Get everyone inside," Tiaki-rangi said quietly. "Now."

But it was already too late.

From the western mountains came a sound like the earth splitting open. A roar that shook the water in the lake, that sent birds exploding from the trees in panicked clouds. And then, movement.

Maunga-kēhua rose.

He moved like a landslide, like an avalanche, like the mountains themselves had decided to walk. Trees snapped like twigs beneath his bulk. Boulders rolled down his sides as he shifted his weight. And his eyes, those terrible prismatic eyes, caught the light of the red moon and began to glow.

Crimson light spilled from his eye sockets like water from a spring. It painted the landscape in shades of blood and shadow. And where that light touched creatures froze.

In the village, Tū-tara was organising the evacuation. "To the boats!" he shouted. "Everyone to the…"

The red light washed over him.

Tū-tara stopped mid-word. His massive body went rigid as stone. His eyes were still open, still aware, but he couldn't move. Couldn't even breathe. The red moon's power, channeled through Maunga-kēhua's ancient eyes, held him in a prison of his own flesh.

From the lake's edge, Kaimana screamed. "No! TŪ-TARA!"

She started running toward him, but Hāwera grabbed her arm. "You can't! The light..."

"I don't care!"

"He would want you to survive!" Hāwera pulled harder, tears streaming down her face. "Kaimana, please!"

Maunga-kēhua moved closer. His tail, a massive, jagged thing covered in stone-like scales. It rose high into the air. It blocked out the moon for a moment, casting a shadow so deep it felt like the end of the world.

Then it fell.

The tail whipped through the air with a sound like thunder. It moved too fast for something so large. It moved with the certainty of a blade, the weight of mountains behind it.

It struck Tū-tara's neck.

The sound was beyond sound. It was the noise of the world breaking.

The shockwave rippled outward in a perfect circle. It flattened trees. It cracked rocks. It sent waves racing across the lake in all directions, water climbing the shores and flooding the forest floor.

And Tū-tara's head, severed clean. Launched into the air.

It rose like a comet. It spun as it flew, catching the moonlight, trailing a spiral of red mist. It sailed over the village, over the gardens, over the sacred lake called Whai-roa-moana. It flew so far and so high that for a moment it seemed it might reach the stars.

Then gravity remembered it, and it fell.

It landed on the highest hill visible from the lake, a prominent peak the people had always called sacred. The head came to rest upright, as though Tū-tara were still standing, still watching over his people. Still guarding them.

The people would later name that hill **Te Pou-tū**, the standing post.

Ririwha's Return

Out in the Pacific Ocean, Ririwha was watching the stars.

She often did this at night. Tracking their movements, noting their patterns, remembering the old stories each constellation held. She was thinking about her grandchildren, wondering if Tiaki-rangi had remembered to bring in the drying racks before the evening dew, when she heard it.

The sound.

Her head snapped toward the land so fast that her movement created a wave that rolled to shore minutes later. Her eyes, warm brown, deep as earth, now widened.

"No," she whispered.

She saw the mushroom cloud of debris rising from Whai-roa-moana. She saw the red moon glowing above it like an evil eye. She saw the curtain of mist that now obscured her family's home.

And she ran.

Each step created tsunamis. Her first stride sent water crashing over the coastal dunes of the eastern bay. Her second flooded the estuaries at the northern coves. Fish and dolphins and stingrays found themselves suddenly in places they'd never been, gasping in newly formed tidal pools.

With one enormous leap, Ririwha cleared the coastal cliffs. She flew through the air for three heartbeats, enough time to see the devastation below, enough time to understand that nothing would ever be the same and then she crashed down into Whai-roa-moana's shallow western arm.

The impact sent water exploding in every direction. A wall of lake spray rose fifty feet high, mixing with the ash and smoke already hanging in the air. The world turned to fog.

Ririwha plunged forward, blind now, wading through the murky depths toward where she'd last seen light. Her foot came down on something, a building, a tree? And then it crumbled beneath her weight.

"Kaimana!" she called. "Tiaki-rangi! Where are you?"

Only echoes answered.

She stumbled forward, hands outstretched, until her fingers struck something. Something large. Something that shouldn't be in the middle of the lake.

The fog cleared for just a moment, and Ririwha looked down.

It was a head. Tū-tara's head. Still upright. Still proud. Still wearing the expression of a chief trying to protect his people.

But so very, very dead.

Ririwha stood there for a long moment. Water lapped at her knees. Ash drifted down like snow. The red moon glared down at the scene with indifference.

Then she tipped her head back and wailed.

The sound was primal. It was the grief of a thousand years compressed into a single note. It was every mother who had lost a child, every elder who had seen their world end, every guardian who had failed their charge.

Birds fell silent. The wind died. Even the lake seemed to still.

And when she finally lowered her head, when her eyes opened again, they were different. The warm brown had mixed with the red of the moon. Her jaw set. Her hands curled into fists.

She began to speak. Her voice was low and formal, words of mourning that had been spoken since the beginning:

"Come forth, grandmothers and grandfathers from the night
Call to those who mourn
Gather our dead to be wept over this day
To all the people, let the call go forth"

As she spoke the last words, the fog parted directly above her. A circle of clear sky opened, and through it the red moon shone down like a spotlight, like an accusation, like a challenge.

Ririwha's jaw snapped shut. Her teeth ground together with the sound of stone on stone.

"MAUNGA-KĒHUA!" she roared. The name echoed across the water, across the mountains, across the very bones of the land. "FACE ME!"

From the western mountains came an answering roar. Defiant. Frustrated. Angry.

The battle had only just begun.

Part Three: Te Whawhai / The Battle

The fog was lifting now, torn apart by the violence of supernatural forces in conflict. Through the clearing air, Ririwha could see the battlefield taking shape.

To the north, where the peaceful bay met the land, something terrible was happening.

Tiaki-rangi stood waist-deep in water, surrounded by dozens of smaller taniwha. They circled him like sharks, their jeweled eyes gleaming, their mouths full of teeth like broken glass. He held a massive **taiaha** (fighting staff) carved from a single kauri tree, his grandfather's grandfather's weapon. His body was covered in cuts, his breathing labored.

But he was still standing. Still fighting.

"Stay back!" he shouted at the taniwha. "I am kaitiaki here! I have rights to this place!"

The taniwha didn't listen. They were beyond listening now, driven by hunger and their father's rage.

One lunged. Tiaki-rangi's taiaha swept around in an arc, connecting with the creature's skull with a crack like lightning. The taniwha fell, stunned. But three more took its place.

"Brother!" Kaimana's voice came from the southern shore. She was trying to reach him, but the water was too deep, too churned up by fighting bodies.

"Go!" Tiaki-rangi called back. "Mother is here! She'll need you! GO!"

Another taniwha struck. Then another. Tiaki-rangi fought like a man possessed, his staff a blur of motion. But there were too many. Far too many.

He was driven back, back, until his shoulders hit the hillside. There was nowhere left to retreat.

The taniwha surged forward as one.

When it was over, when the water finally cleared, Tiaki-rangi remained. But he would never leave that place.

His body had become part of the hillside itself, back pressed against the earth, face still turned toward the village he'd protected. His eyes were closed now, but his expression was peaceful. As though in his last moment, he'd understood something important.

The land had welcomed him home. He was kaitiaki still. He would always be kaitiaki.

The people would later call that place **Maunga-tiaki**, Guardian Mountain and they would visit it when they needed courage. When they needed to remember that some things are worth fighting for.

The Guardian's Sacrifice

Kaimana heard her son's last battle cry fade into silence. She stopped running. Stopped breathing for a moment. The world contracted to a single point of pain so sharp it was almost physical.

"No," she whispered. "Not him. Not my boy."

But the smell of smoke and blood told her the truth.

She was standing at the edge of the lake, near the path that led up through the dense jungle toward the eastern streams. Behind her, the sounds of battle continued. Ahead, the forest was dark and tangled and safe.

Hāwera appeared beside her, breathing hard. "We have to move. Now. While they're distracted."

"My son is dead."

"I know." Hāwera's voice cracked. "Tū-tara is dead too. But we can't join them. We can't. Your mother needs us to survive."

Kaimana looked back one last time at the chaos. At the red moon hanging over it all like a curse. At her mother wading through the deep water toward the source of all this pain.

Then she ran.

Ririwha had reached the western arm of Whai-roa-moana now, moving through the deeper water toward where she knew Maunga-kēhua must be. The red light still pulsed from the mountains, but it was dimmer now. The moon's power was fading as it rose higher in the sky.

She had to end this. Now. While she still could.

"Where are you, old monster?" she called. "Where…"

The water exploded.

Maunga-kēhua erupted from beneath the surface like a nightmare made solid. His massive head broke through first, water cascading off scales as thick as shield walls. His mouth opened, too wide, lined with teeth in the wrong places. He roared directly into Ririwha's face.

The sound hit her like a physical force. But she didn't flinch.

"You killed my son-in-law," she said quietly. "You've destroyed my home. You've broken every covenant, every agreement our ancestors made."

Maunga-kēhua's prismatic eyes focused on her. In their depths, she could see madness. Hunger and something else, desperation.

"Your family hoarded while mine starved," the ancient creature rumbled. His voice was the sound of mountains grinding together. "Your precious birds, your careful balance. What about MY children?"

"Your children broke the balance!" Ririwha shot back. "They took more than they needed! They…"

Ririwha rose from the crimson-lit waters of the great lake like a force born from the earth itself. Waist-high in the swirling current, her massive form towered above the foaming waves, muscles coiled beneath skin streaked with ash and reflected flame. Her long, wet hair clung to her back, whipping about in the volcanic wind as the distant mountains rumbled like drums of war. Above them, the sky burned red. A blood moon hanging low over the erupting peaks, spilling ember-light across the land. Every breath she drew sent ripples rolling across the lake's surface.

Opposite her, the taniwha Maunga-kēhua. The creature was vast, its armored scales blackened by ash. Its glowing eyes like burning coals beneath the shadow of the volcano. When it moved, the lake heaved. When it rose, water fled from its body as if terrified to cling to it. Its jaws, wide enough to swallow a waka whole, snapped at her in fury, and the sound echoed across the hills like the crack of thunder.

Surging forward, reaching for her neck, for the pounamu (greenstone) necklace she'd worn for a thousand years. A gift from her own mother, carved from stone as old as the islands themselves. She ripped it free, meeting the taniwha head-on.

She drove her hands into the water, pushing herself through the churning waves as Maunga-kēhua circled her, its serpentine body coiling beneath the surface. Steam hissed around them where molten ash rained upon the lake turning the air thick, hot, and heavy with the scent of scorched earth. Their battle churned the shallows into a violent whirlpool, water exploding upward with every blow, every impact, every clash of flesh against ancient scale.

With a roar of her own, Ririwha lunged as the taniwha darted past, her fingers brushing the ridged plates along its spine. The creature twisted, its tail whipping around in a surge that broke like a tidal wave against her chest. She staggered but did not fall. Planting her feet deep into the lakebed, she straightened, towering over the waves once more. All around them the mountains trembled, the volcanoes belched fire. The sky burned as two giants fought. one made of myth, whilst the other was mostly formed by legends.

They both continued to skirmish for dominance in the heart of the trembling land.

Maunga-kēhua finally got a hold of Ririwha, with his massive jaws. Giving him the upper hand as they snapped shut around her right ankle. His teeth, each one as long as a waka, pierced through flesh, through muscle, grinding against bone.

Ririwha screamed.

As she began to thrusting her mighty green stone necklace like a dagger, stabbing it downward, again and again. Driving the sharp edge into Maunga-kēhua's snout, his eyes, anything she could reach.

Green stone met scales. Sparks flew. The water around them began to glow with a strange light, the power of the stone recognizing the power of the creature.

Maunga-kēhua bellowed in pain but didn't let go. Instead, he began to swim in a circle, using his massive body as leverage, pulling Ririwha off balance.

She fell.

The impact was cataclysmic.

Ririwha's body, 2,930 metres of living mountain, crashed backward into the thin strip of land that separated Whai-roa-moana from the ocean. The coastal barrier, hundreds of feet of rock and earth that had stood since the land first rose from the sea, the ground crumbled beneath her weight.

Stone's shattered. Earth gave way. And the ocean came rushing in.

The Breaking of the Land

The sea met the lake with a roar louder than any living thing could make.

Water poured through the new breach in a churning, frothing torrent. Seawater and freshwater collided, mixed, creating whirlpools and eddies and currents that had never existed before. The lake level began to drop as water rushed out. The sea level rose as water rushed in.

Whai-roa-moana was dying. And from its death, something new was being born.

The taniwha felt the change immediately. The added salt content burned their sensitive gills. They were freshwater creatures, adapted to the pure lake, and the ocean's salinity was poison to them. They began to retreat, swimming frantically back toward the western mountains, toward the streams and caves where they could survive.

But they were trapped now. The lake was becoming a harbour. The harbour would open to the sea. There would be no going back.

Some of the taniwha made it to the tunnels beneath the coastal rocks before the transformation was complete. They burrowed deep, finding pockets of fresh water filtered through stone. They would hibernate there, dormant, waiting.

Others weren't so lucky.

Ririwha lay on her back, half in the new harbour, half floating out toward the open ocean. Blood clouded the water around her. Her right ankle was mangled, torn, useless. The pain was enormous, but somehow distant, as though it were happening to someone else.

She could feel herself drifting. Feel the tide pulling her out to sea.

"Kaimana," she whispered. "Tiaki-rangi."

No one answered.

The red moon was setting now, replaced by the gentle pre-dawn light. The battle was over. The world had changed. And Ririwha was so, so tired.

She let the current take her. It carried her gently past the newly formed harbour entrance, out into the open ocean. The water was cooler here, clearer. She could see stars reflecting off the sea's surface.

Eventually, she came to rest on a reef. A place where the water was shallow and warm, where small fish darted between coral formations, where the sun would soon rise and paint everything gold.

Ririwha closed her eyes.

"I'm sorry," she whispered to the sky, to her children, to the land itself. "I'm so sorry."

The first ray of dawn touched her face.

And the ancient guardian was still.

Part Four: Te Whakamaumahara / The Remembering

High on the hills above the transformed harbour, a figure stood frozen.

Kaimana had made it to this place, to the heights where she could see everything. The transformed harbour, wider now, deeper, forever changed. The reef where her mother lay. The hills where her son had fallen. The mountain where her husband's head rested, noble even in death.

She stood there, looking out, and the weight of grief turned her to stone.

Not slowly. Not metaphorically. Actually, truly to stone.

Her feet rooted into the earth. Her body hardened, transformed, becoming part of the ridge itself. Her face remained turned toward the sea, toward her mother, keeping an eternal vigil.

The people would call her formation **Te Ihu-o-te-rangi**, the nose of heaven. This monument would remind them that she was watching. Always watching. Still keeping guard.

Hāwera had run in a different direction.

When the water began to change, when she realized the lake was becoming something else, she'd fled east. Through the thick undergrowth, following half-remembered trails, until she burst out onto a different shore entirely.

Before her lay scattered islands, jewels of stone and forest floating in the blue Pacific. Behind her lay a world that no longer existed. A home that had drowned.

She sat down on the shore and wept until she had no tears left.

Then she built a small whare (house) from driftwood and harakeke. She planted a garden. She learned to fish in the saltwater, to gather kina and pāua from the rocks. She survived.

And sometimes, on clear nights when the moon was dark and the stars were bright, she would walk to the water's edge and look west. Toward where Whai-roa-moana used to be. Toward where her husband's head still stood on its hill, watching over nothing.

"I remember," she would whisper to the waves. "I remember all of it."

The people would say that Hāwera lived for another three hundred years before she too became part of the land. A small peak near the eastern islands, still looking west, still remembering.

The Names That Remain

Time passed, as it always does.

The harbour that had been Whai-roa-moana was given a new name. The people who came after the transformation called it **Te Whanga-ā-Rua**, the harbour of the chasm. For the way the ocean had torn through the land to claim it.

Tū-tara's head, resting on its sacred hill, was named **Te Pou-tū**, the standing post. Travelers would look up at it from their waka and remember the chief who had tried to protect his people.

Tiaki-rangi's resting place became **Maunga-tiaki**, Guardian Mountain. Where he fell defending the northern bay. Fishermen would leave offerings there even centuries later, though many had forgotten why.

Ririwha herself became an island chain.

The reef where she died rose and fell with the tides, eventually breaking the surface permanently. Trees grew on her back. Birds nested in her hair. She became **Motu-tūpuna**, ancestor island, a place of sanctuary and remembrance.

And Kaimana, faithful daughter, eternal watcher, stood vigil on her hill. **Te Ihu-o-te-rangi**, the nose of heaven, her profile forever etched against the sky.

The Taniwha's Dream

Deep beneath the rocky islands where the waves break eternal, in tunnels honeycomb through ancient stone, the surviving taniwha sleep.

They are not dead. Not quite.

Their breathing is so slow that a single breath takes a year. Their hearts beat once per lunar month. They lie in cold mud and filtered fresh water, their massive bodies coiled in the dark.

They dream of the red moon. They dream of the taste of vengeance. They dream of a world where their father's rage was justified.

And they wait.

Because the taniwha know something that humans often forget: time is patient. Time is long. And grudges, like stones, are eternal.

Local kaumātua still warn children not to swim near certain rocks. Not to dive in certain places. Because you never know, they say. You never know what might be sleeping beneath.

In the same tunnels, if you look carefully, you might find other inhabitants now. The **tuatara**. Living fossils, ancient reptiles that have survived everything the world has thrown at them. And the **tītī** (muttonbirds) who nest in the burrows, unaware they share their homes with sleeping monsters.

It's a strange sort of coexistence. But it works, as most things in nature eventually do.

The End.

<u>Epilogue</u>: Te Ao Hurihuri - The Changing World

Today, if you visit the harbours of Te Tai Tokerau (Northland) in Aotearoa, you'll find places of striking beauty.

Deep channels reach into the land like fingers. The water runs deep and clear. Boats bob at anchor. Children swim from the docks. Kingfishers hunt in the shallows.

On a clear day, you can see islands on the horizon. You can see distinctive rock formations rising above the shores. You can see all the hills and bays that might have inspired stories like this one.

If you're lucky, if you're quiet and respectful and you go at the right time. You might see kororā (little blue penguins) darting through the water. You might spot an ancient leatherback turtle cruising through the harbour. You might watch a pōhutukawa tree drop its red flowers into the water, where they float away on the current like memory itself, still drifting after all these years.

The people who live there now are the descendants of many ethnicities. Māori, Pākehā, and others. They fish the same waters. They walk the same hills. They live under the same stars.

Some still remember the old stories. The real ones, passed down through generations by those who have mana whenua over these lands. Some still leave offerings at certain places. Some still teach their children the proper karakia before fishing in certain spots. Some still feel the weight of watching from the hills.

Because guardianship never really ends. It transforms, like everything else. It becomes something deeper. Something that lasts not just for a lifetime, bu for all the lifetimes to come.

This is what kaitiakitanga means. Not just protecting what is, but honoring what was, and safeguarding what will be.

He Waiata Whakakitenga - A Song of Vision

A fictional waiata created for this story:

Titiro ki ngā maunga, e tū tonu rā
(Look to the mountains, still standing)

Whakarongo ki te moana, e tangi tonu rā
(Listen to the ocean, still calling)

Kei konei tonu ngā kaitiaki
(The guardians are still here)

Kei roto i te whenua, kei roto i te wai
(In the land, in the waters)

Kei roto i ō tātou ngākau
(In our hearts)

Tiakina te taiao
(Protect the environment)

Mō āpōpō, mō ngā uri
(For tomorrow, for the descendants)

Kia ora te ao
(So the world may thrive)

www.ingramcontent.com/pod-product-compliance
Lightning Source LLC
Chambersburg PA
CBHW020535120726
47904CB00003B/1096